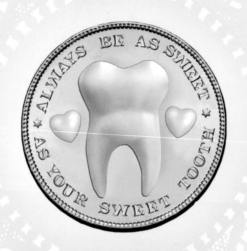

Silverlicious

WRITTEN AND ILLUSTRATED
BY Victoria Kann

HARPER
An Imprint of HarperCollinsPublishers

Library of Congress Cataloging-in-Publication Data
Kann, Victoria.
Silverlicious / written and illustrated by Victoria Kann. — 1st ed.
p. cm.
Summary: When Pinkalicious loses her sweet tooth, she turns to the Tooth Fairy for help.
ISBN 978-0-06-178123-0 (trade bdg.) — ISBN 978-0-06-178124-7 (lib. bdg.)
[1. Tooth Fairy—Fiction. 2. Teeth—Fiction. 3. Brothers and sisters—Fiction.] I. Title.
PZ7.K127745i 2010   2009049487   [E]—dc22   CIP   AC

Typography by Rachel Zegar
11 12 13 14 15   CG/WOR   10 9 8 7 6 5 4 3 2 1
❖
First Edition

Thank you
Christina, Leigha,
David & Patricia
for your artistic
contribution.

I had a wiggly tooth. It had been wiggling for days.

I wiggled my tooth at breakfast and I wiggled it at lunch. At snack time I saw that Peter was eating a chocolicious cookie.

I grabbed it and took a big bite.

"Look, my tooth came out! YAY!" I said, but something was wrong.

"OH, NO, MOMMY! It wasn't just ANY tooth—it was my SWEET TOOTH! This cookie has no flavor. It tastes like . . . dirt!"

"Oh dear! You lost your sweet tooth?" asked Mommy.

"How dreadful!" said Daddy.

"That's what you get for stealing my cookie!" said Peter, sniffling.

"What am I going to do without my sweet tooth?"

"I know. . . ." I grabbed my pinkatastic pen and started to write:

Dear Tooth Fairy,

Today my sweet tooth came out. What should I do? Could you please send me something sweet to eat until a new tooth grows in?

Love,
Pinkalicious

I tucked the note under my pillow with my tooth and kept one eye open all night. I had always wanted to know exactly what the tooth fairy looks like. Tonight I would see her!

Piiiiiiink . . . piiiiiiiink . . . . . . piiiiiiiiiiink went my alarm. I must have fallen asleep! I looked for my tooth, but it was gone. In its place were three red candy hearts and a note.

Dearest Pinkalicious,

How art thou? Tootheetina, your personal tooth fairy, was busy last night. Unfortunately a girl in New Zealand was having her molars out. Tootheetina had to fly there to help her. It takes a long time for a tooth fairy to fly, because her wings are so small. Tootheetina asked me to help you. I hope you don't mind.

Forever yours,

Carlos Cupid

"Peter, come quick!" I shouted. "Cupid was here!"

"Did you see him? Did you? Did you?" asked Peter.

"No, I missed him. I guess I fell asleep. Look—he left me candy." I put a couple of red hearts in my mouth. "EEEEEEEEEEEKKKKKK! These are red hots! My mouth is burning!" I yelled. "They taste like coal!"

"Yum! They taste great to me," said Peter. "And look at all the hearts in your room. Cupid must really like you."

"Cupid loves EVERYBODY! Where is my tooth fairy? I want MY TOOTH FAIRY!" I said, stomping my foot.

My plan was to stay awake all night long so I could take a picture of Cupid to show my class. I had my camera ready! I wrote another note:

Dear Carlos Cupid,

Thank you so much for the red hots. Unfortunately THEY WERE DISGUSTING!!!! I would prefer to have something sweet.

Love,

Pinkalicious

Piiiiink . . . piiiiiink . . . . . . piiiiiiiiink went my alarm. I had fallen asleep again! I looked for my note. It was gone! In its place were three jelly beans and a new note.

When I tasted the jelly beans, they felt like little pebbles in my mouth. "YUCK!" I said, spitting them out. "These jelly beans taste awful! And look at all the footprints the bunny left around my room!" I complained.

"I don't see anything wrong with it at all," said Peter. "Looks like he left eggs everywhere!" He grabbed a basket and started to collect as many as he could.

Where is Tootheetina? I wondered.

That night I wrote another note. I had my camera ready, plus a net so I could catch that Bunny if he had the nerve to hop around my room again. I would definitely stay awake tonight.

Dear Edgar Easter Bunny,
Thank you so much for the eggs. Unfortunately I lost my sweet tooth, so the jelly beans HAD NO FLAVOR! Could you Please, Please, Please ask Tootheetina to come and leave me something sweet? Love,
Pinkalicious

Piiiiink . . . piiiiiink . . . . . piiiiiiiink went my alarm.
I fell asleep AGAIN! This time I found three tiny candy
canes and a note.

Dear Pinkalicious,
   I am so happy that I got
a break from all the toys I
have to make, morning, noon
and night. Being a tooth fairy
is a much better job!
   Tootheetina had to fly to
Japan to celebrate with a little
boy who was finally getting
his braces off. She asked me
to help out.
Have a very merry day!
   elf #351

I licked a candy cane. "GROSS!" It tasted just like hard toothpaste.
"What a mess!" There was snow everywhere.
"Do you think he left some toys here too?" asked Peter. "You sure
are lucky! When I lose a tooth, I just get a few coins under my pillow."

"But I wanted something sweet from the tooth fairy.
Something that would taste good until my new sweet tooth
grows in. I want Tootheetina."

That night I was ready.

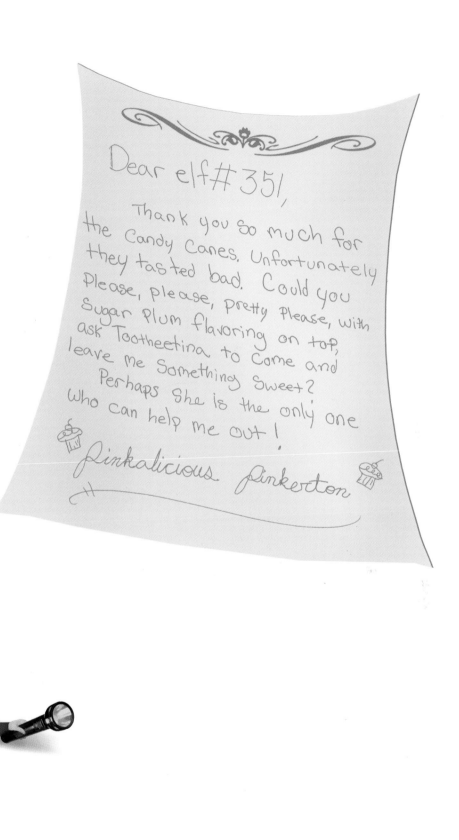

Dear elf #351,

Thank you so much for the Candy Canes. Unfortunately they tasted bad. Could you please, please, pretty please, with Sugar Plum flavoring on top, ask Tootheetina to come and leave me something sweet? Perhaps she is the only one who can help me out!

Pinkalicious Pinkerton

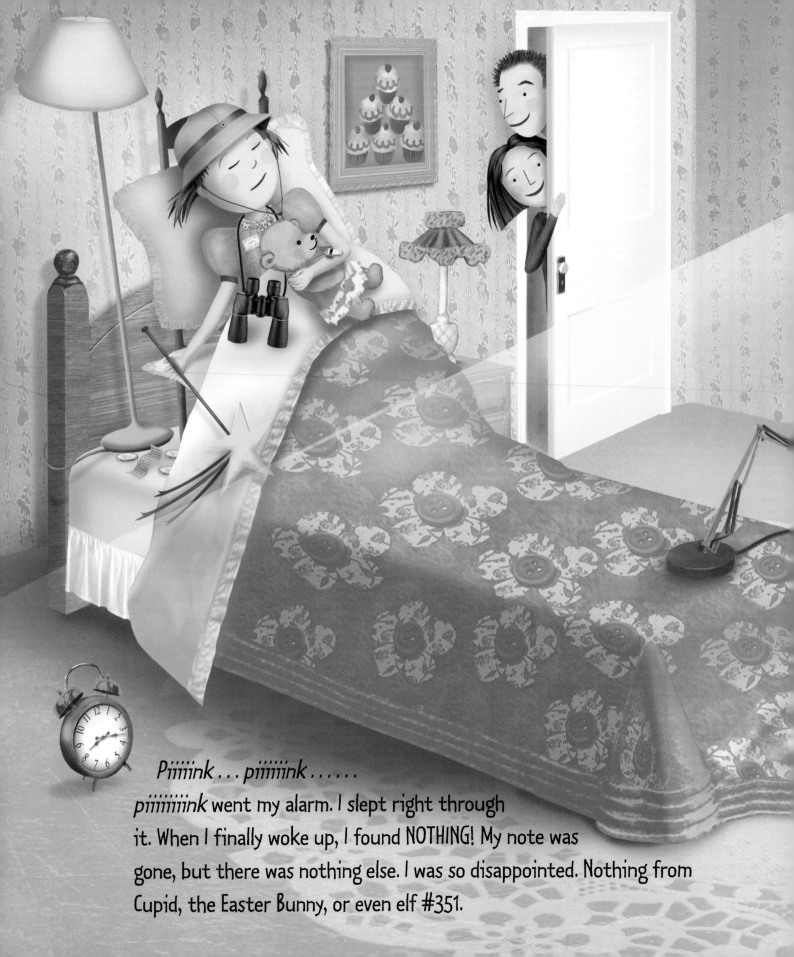

Piiiiink . . . piiiiiink . . . . . .
piiiiiiiink went my alarm. I slept right through
it. When I finally woke up, I found NOTHING! My note was
gone, but there was nothing else. I was so disappointed. Nothing from
Cupid, the Easter Bunny, or even elf #351.

Then I noticed a teeny weeny slip of paper under my chair and three silver coins.

Dear Pinkalicious,
Sweetness comes from the inside. When you are sweet, the world and all the delicious things in it will be sweet too!
With love,
Tootheetina
P.S. Don't forget to brush and floss after every meal!

Huh? What does THAT mean? I wondered. Hadn't I been sweet?
Maybe I wasn't sweet when I bit into Peter's chocolicious cookie
or stomped my feet or spit out the candy. Maybe I could have been
sweeter to Cupid, the Easter Bunny, and elf #351. I was really very
lucky that they came and visited me. I wrote a new note:

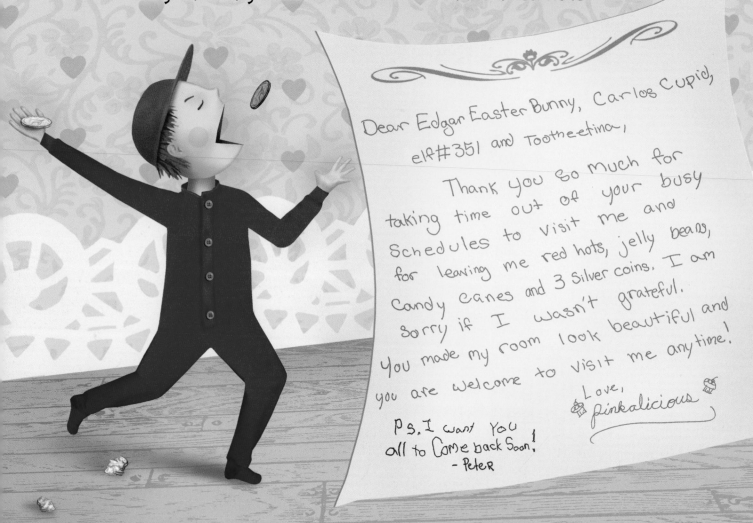

Dear Edgar Easter Bunny, Carlos Cupid,
elf #351 and Tootheetina,

Thank you so much for
taking time out of your busy
schedules to visit me and
for leaving me red hots, jelly beans,
candy canes and 3 silver coins. I am
sorry if I wasn't grateful.
You made my room look beautiful and
you are welcome to visit me anytime!
Love,
Pinkalicious

P.S. I want you
all to come back soon!
- Peter

I folded it up for later. I began to feel much better.
"Hey, Pinkalicious, did you know that the silver coins are
actually made of chocolate?" asked Peter, stealing the coins out of
my hand and running around the room.

"Peter, you can have the chocolates because you are USUALLY such a nice brother," I said sweetly.

"Huh? Um . . . I don't want them. You can have them back. I'm sorry I took them," Peter said, handing them back to me.

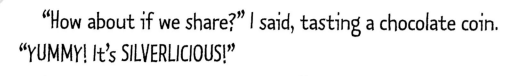

"How about if we share?" I said, tasting a chocolate coin. "YUMMY! It's SILVERLICIOUS!"

I can taste sweet things again! Hooray! From now on I am always going to be as sweet as my sweet tooth.